ANITA LOBEL

Lena's Sleep Sheep
A Going-to-Bed Book

Alfred A. Knopf
New York

$\mathcal{L}$ena was cozy in bed.
Mama and Papa hugged and
kissed her good night.

"Please don't close the curtains, Papa," Lena said.
"The moon is nice and round tonight."

"Won't it keep you awake?" asked Mama.

"No," said Lena. "He will keep me company."

"Until my sheep come," she thought.
"They will like his sweet face, too."

As soon as Mama and Papa left,
Lena whispered, "Come out, come out, my woolly friends!
I'm ready to count you now.
One sheep, two sheep, three sheep . . . ," she began.

But tonight, something was not right.
Lena's sleep sheep would not line up.

"Why are you hiding from me?" Lena asked.

"We're sca-a-a-a-red!" the sheep baa-a-a-a-ed together.

"What are you scared of?" she asked.

"There's a round monster in the window,
making faces at us!" they cried.
"He looks hungry and ready for a sheep snack."

"You silly sheep," Lena laughed.

"That round thing is not a monster.
It is the moon in the night sky.
He's not hungry. He's already full."

But the sheep were still scared.

"I have to do something about this,"
Lena thought.

Then Lena had a good idea.
"Listen, sheep friends," she said. "Go into my closet.
You will find clothes to dress up in.
The moon will not know you are sheep."

The sheep did as they were told.
They found all sorts of fun things to wear.
Hidden in Lena's clothes,
they were not scared anymore.

"You clever sheep, you!" Lena said.
"Now, please go to work!

"One sheep, two sheep, three sheep, four sheep, fi—"
Lena stopped counting.

The sheep were clumsy in their costumes.
They were baa-ing and bleating and bumping into each other.

"This isn't working!" Lena cried.

Then something happened.
One of the sheep pointed at the window.
"Look, look! The round monster is gone!" she baa-a-a-a-ed.

Lena saw that the moon had slipped behind a cloud.
"Stay there for now, good moon," she thought.

"Clever sheep!" Lena said.
"You scared the monster away.
Now you can get out of your disguises
and help me fall asleep."

The sheep took off their costumes.

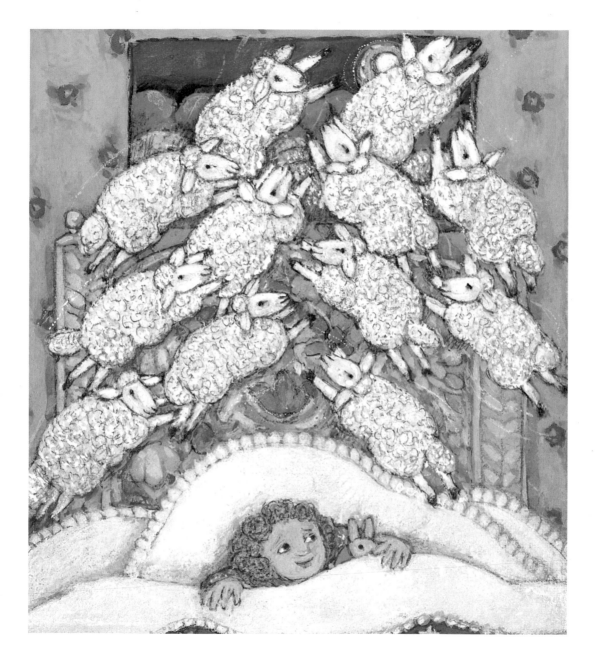

Light as air, they rose up to form a nice, neat line above the bed.

Lena began to count.
"One sheep, two sheep, three sheep, four . . . five . . . six . . . seven . . .
eight . . . ," she mumbled. "Nine . . . ten . . . eleve . . . e . . . e . . . n . . ."
She did not even get to twelve
before she fell fast asleep.

Peeking out from behind his cloud,
the moon seemed to whisper,
"Good night, silly sheep.
And good night, lovely Lena."

THIS IS A BORZOI BOOK PUBLISHED BY ALFRED A. KNOPF

Visit us on the Web! randomhouse.com/kids

Educators and librarians, for a variety of teaching tools, visit us at RHTeachersLibrarians.com

Library of Congress Cataloging-in-Publication Data
Lobel, Anita.
Lena's sleep sheep : a going-to-bed book / Anita Lobel. — 1st ed.
p. cm.
Summary: Lena wants the sheep she counts at bedtime to meet another of her nighttime friends, but they think the moon is a monster and are afraid.
ISBN 978-0-449-81025-5 (trade) — ISBN 978-0-449-81026-2 (lib. bdg.) —
ISBN 978-0-449-81027-9 (ebook)
[1. Bedtime—Fiction. 2. Sheep—Fiction. 3. Moon—Fiction.] I. Title.
PZ7.L7794Len 2013
[E]—dc23
2012028378

The text of this book is set in 15-point Bookman.
The illustrations were created using gouache and watercolor.
MANUFACTURED IN MALAYSIA
August 2013
10 9 8 7 6 5 4 3 2 1
First Edition